MAGIC BONE

BONE

NEVER BOX WITH A KANGAROO

For Amanda and Ian, who have never fit into boxes.
And have never wanted to—NK

For Nick and Karen—SB

GROSSET & DUNLAP
Penguin Young Readers Group
An Imprint of Penguin Random House LLC

If you purchased this book without a cover, you should be aware that this book is stolen property. It was reported as "unsold and destroyed" to the publisher, and neither the author nor the publisher has received any payment for this "stripped book."

Penguin supports copyright. Copyright fuels creativity, encourages diverse voices, promotes free speech, and creates a vibrant culture. Thank you for buying an authorized edition of this book and for complying with copyright laws by not reproducing, scanning, or distributing any part of it in any form without permission. You are supporting writers and allowing Penguin to continue to publish books for every reader.

The publisher does not have any control over and does not assume any responsibility for author or third-party websites or their content.

Text copyright © 2016 by Nancy Krulik. Illustrations copyright © 2016 by Sebastien Braun. All rights reserved. Published by Grosset & Dunlap, an imprint of Penguin Random House LLC, 345 Hudson Street, New York, New York 10014. GROSSET & DUNLAP is a trademark of Penguin Random House LLC. Printed in the USA.

Library of Congress Cataloging-in-Publication Data is available.

ISBN 9780448488769   10 9 8 7 6 5 4 3 2 1

WITHDRAWN

MAGIC BONE

NEVER BOX WITH A KANGAROO

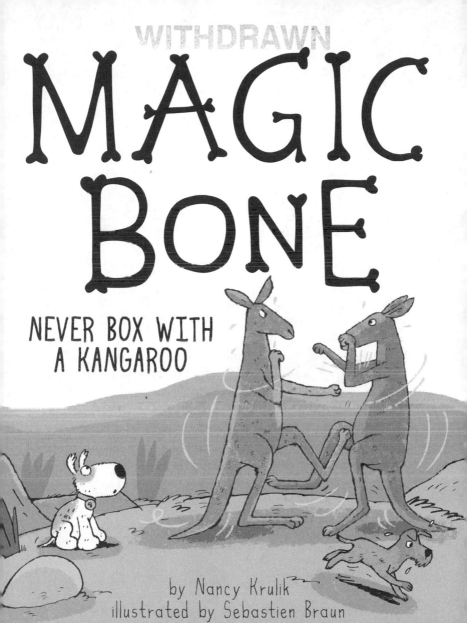

by Nancy Krulik
illustrated by Sebastien Braun

Grosset & Dunlap
An Imprint of Penguin Random House

CHAPTER 1

"I've got it! I've got it!" I bark excitedly.

I'm chasing after a ball in the air.

My paws speed up. Now I am running. Fast. Faster. *Fastest.*

My eyes are following the ball as it soars above me.

"I'm gonna catch you!" I bark to the ball.

Plop. The ball hits the ground.

The ball was too fast for me . . . this time. But I'll get it next time!

I scoop up the ball in my mouth and bring it back to my two-leg, Josh. Now we can play again.

I love when Josh brings me to the park. It's bigger than our yard. There's much more room to run.

"Here's the ball!" I bark. "Throw it again! I'll catch it this time."

Suddenly, I hear puppies talking. *Lots of them.*

"Look at me!" one squeals.

"No, look at *me*!" yips another.

"I can roll in the grass," a third puppy barks.

"I'm hungry," whines the littlest one.

There are four puppies playing by a tree. A bigger dog is standing nearby with her two-leg.

Wiggle, waggle, weird. All those puppies look alike. I've never seen four friends who look so much like one another.

Those puppies are having fun rolling around in the grass. I want to play, too!

"Can I play?" I bark to the puppies.

Before they can answer me, Josh snaps my leash around my neck. He starts to lead me out of the park.

"I don't want to go!" I bark to Josh. "I want to play with the other puppies."

But Josh keeps leading me out of the park. He doesn't understand what I am saying. That's because Josh doesn't speak dog. And I don't speak two-leg.

I will have to show him that I don't want to leave.

I flop down on my belly. I dig my paws into the ground.

I'm not leaving.

Josh gives me a funny look. I give him a funny look back. Then he gives me another funny look.

I like this game!

Suddenly, Josh drops my leash. He starts to walk away.

Uh-oh! Is Josh leaving me here?

"Don't leave me, Josh!" I bark. Then I run to him.

Josh smiles. He takes my leash. And we go home together.

When we get to our house, Josh puts me in the yard. Then he closes the gate and leaves me all alone. Boo!

Vroom. Vroom.

That's the sound of Josh's big

metal machine with the four round paws going away.

I wonder where Josh is going. I bet it's somewhere fun.

No fair! I want to go somewhere fun, too!

Hey. Wait a minute. I *can* go somewhere fun. And I don't need a metal machine to do it.

I run over to the part of my yard where the flowers grow, and I start *diggety, dig, digging.* I'm a *great* digger.

Diggety, dig, dig. Dirt flies everywhere. The hole gets bigger and bigger. And then . . . *there it is!* My beautiful, sparkly white bone. Just where I buried it.

"Hello, bone!" I bark.

My bone doesn't answer. That's because bones can't bark. Not even a special bone like this one.

My bone isn't just any bone. It's a magic bone. It takes me places. All I have to do is take a bite and—*kaboom*—off I go!

The first time I took a trip with my magic bone, I went to London, England. London had yummy food like fish and chips. But London also had a scary place called the pound. I got thrown in there, and it was no fun at all. There were some mean dogs in the pound.

Another time, my magic bone took me to Paris, France, where I got to dance in paint and eat yummy treats called croissants.

Then there was the day my bone *kaboomed* me to New York City. It was really crowded there. And they have mean pigeons who try to steal your food. But I got to eat a New York hot dog—which is actually not a dog at all.

Sniff . . . sniff . . . sniff. My bone smells so meaty. I just have to take a bite.

CHOMP!

Wiggle, waggle, whew. I feel dizzy—like my insides are spinning all around—but my outsides are standing still. Stars are twinkling in front of my eyes—even though it's daytime! All around me I smell food—fried chicken, salmon, roast beef. But there isn't any food in sight.

Kaboom! Kaboom! Kaboom!

CHAPTER 2

Wiggle, waggle, where am I?

I look around. I'm standing right by a tall tree.

Grunt!

Wow! I've never heard a tree make a noise before!

Grunt.

I look up. There's something furry curled up in the branches. I bet it's what was making that noise.

The only furry things I've ever seen in trees are squirrels. And sometimes Queenie the meanie, our neighborhood cat.

But that thing doesn't look like a squirrel. Or a cat.

Snort!

It doesn't sound like a squirrel or a cat, either. It just sounds angry!

I don't think the furry thing likes me hanging around under its tree.

I want to get away from the angry furry thing. But first I have to bury my bone.

Diggety, dig, dig. I hurry to dig a hole near the bottom of the tree. *Diggety, dig, dig.*

I drop my bone into the hole. Then I *pushity, push, push* the dirt back over it.

No other dog will be able to find

my bone and steal it. When I want to find my bone again, all I will have to do is look for the tree that has an angry furry thing sleeping in its branches.

Now I'm ready to have some fun!

"I want my mummy."

I hear someone whimpering in the nearby bushes, and I can understand what that someone is saying. Which can only mean one thing: Whatever is hiding in the bushes is a *dog*. And he sounds very sad.

I really want to get far away from the loud, snorting furry thing in the tree. But I can't leave when there's a dog in trouble. Dogs have to help each other out.

I wander over to the bushes.

There's a teeny terrier puppy hiding in them. He's shaking all over.

"Don't worry," I tell him. "That furry thing is loud. But I don't think he will hurt us. I think he just wants to scare us away from his tree."

The terrier puppy looks up. "You mean that koala?" he asks. "He's not scaring me."

"Then why are you crying?" I ask him.

"Because I'm never going to see my mummy or my sisters again," he tells me.

"Your *what*?" I ask him.

"My family," he says. "You know."

No, I *don't* know.

"Don't you live with anyone?" the terrier asks.

"Oh yes," I reply. "My two-leg, Josh."

"No other dogs?" he asks.

"Nope," I say.

"Crikey!" the terrier exclaims. "That's strange."

I don't like being called strange. Or *crikey*. Whatever that means.

"Don't you have a two-leg?" I ask him.

"No," he tells me. "It's always been just us dogs."

"Just dogs? Living all alone in a house?"

The terrier shakes his head. "We don't live in a house. We live under a bridge. At least we did, until a two-leg came by and grabbed my mummy and my sisters."

"But he didn't grab you?" I ask him.

"No, I was too fast for him. I ran away and hid."

"You were smart to run away," I tell him. "That two-leg might have been a dogcatcher."

"A what?" he asks me.

"A dogcatcher," I say again. "A two-leg who puts dogs in the pound.

Trust me: You *don't* want to go there."

The terrier gives me a scared look. "Will my mummy and sisters be okay in the pound?"

I do not want to frighten this puppy. He looks scared enough. So I say, "Sure." Even though I'm not sure at all.

The terrier doesn't say anything. He just stands there, shaking. I can tell he's really frightened.

So am I. Because if there's a dogcatcher around, he could be looking to catch more dogs. Like *me*.

"How far is your bridge from here?" I ask the terrier nervously.

"Really far," he tells me. "Across a puddle of water that's so big, you can't even see the whole thing."

Phew. That's too far for that dogcatcher to come looking for us.

But it's also too far for a dog to swim or walk across. This doesn't make any sense. "Then how did you get *here*?" I ask.

"When I ran off, I looked for a place to hide," he tells me. "I found a giant metal machine and climbed inside. The next thing I knew, it was floating on the water! And I wound up here."

"That's scary!" I say.

The teeny terrier nods. *"Real* scary. Because now I'm all alone."

His tail sinks between his legs. His ears droop. He looks so sad.

"You're not alone," I say, trying to cheer him up. "You're with me. My name is Sparky. What's yours?"

"Mick." The terrier smiles at me. "I'm glad you came along, mate."

"Sparky," I correct him.

He looks at me funny. "What?"

"My name's not Mate," I say. "It's Sparky. I just told you that."

The terrier laughs. "Sparky,

you're a real dag," he says.

"No. I'm a *dog*," I tell him. "A *sheep*dog."

Mick laughs again. "I just meant you're a funny guy. A dag. Anyway, now that you're here, I feel better. We can spend all our time together."

Uh-oh. I know that's not true. In a little while, I'm going back to Josh.

Which will leave Mick all alone.

Except that wouldn't be nice. Dogs are supposed to help each other out.

I don't know what to do. This is *baddy, bad, bad.*

"Maybe we can find you a family of dogs here," I say.

Mick gives me a funny look. "Are you crackers?" he asks.

"No, I'm *Sparky*, remember?" I reply.

Mick shakes his head. "I told you, my family isn't here," he says. "They're on the other side of that giant puddle. Far, far away."

"I know," I tell him. "But maybe we can find you a *new* dog family. One where everyone talks the funny way you do."

"I don't talk funny," Mick answers. "Everybody in Australia talks this way."

I guess Australia must be the name of this place.

"We could find you a mummy and some brothers and sisters," I continue. "That way you could have a big family. Then you won't ever be alone."

"A *new* family?" Mick cocks his head sideways. Now *he* is *thinkety, think, thinking*. "But I like my old family. They played with me, and they took care of me . . ."

"Do you think they want you to be happy?" I ask him.

Mick nods. "Mummy always likes when my tail wags."

"Wouldn't you be happier in a family than just wandering around here?" I ask.

Mick's tail wags a little. "I guess it's worth a try," he finally says.

"Come on, Mick," I say. "Let's go find you a family!"

CHAPTER 3

"G'day, mates!" a big shepherd dog barks to us a little while later as we pass a small house.

The shepherd is lying down outside. There's another shepherd right next to her.

This house has flowers and a big tree in the yard. It reminds me of *my* house. I am happy in my house. Maybe Mick can be happy here.

"This is it!" I bark to Mick. "This is your new home."

Mick looks at the house.

And the tree.

And the two shepherds.

His ears perk up. His tail starts to wag.

I think he likes this place.

"Hi," I say to the two shepherds. "My name is Sparky. This is my friend Mick."

"G'day," the bigger of the two shepherds says. "I'm Callie. And this is Ollie."

Ollie comes over and sniffs my butt to say hello. I sniff him right back.

"Are you part of a family?" I ask Callie and Ollie.

"Sure we are," Callie replies. "Isn't everyone?"

Mick's ears flop. His tail sags.

"I had a family once," he says quietly.

"You could find a *new* family," I whisper back. "If you try." I give him a little nudge with my nose.

Slowly, Mick walks over to the shepherds. "Will you be my family?" he asks them.

"I would love that, mate," Ollie says.

My tail starts wagging like crazy. It is so happy to hear that. Which is strange, because my tail doesn't have ears.

"But we can't," Callie adds.

My tail stops wagging.

"Why not?" I ask her.

"Because families can only have two dogs on Kangaroo Island," she explains. "It's a rule."

"Kangaroo Island?" I look at Mick. "I thought you said this place was called Australia."

"Kangaroo Island is part of Australia," Callie explains. "Not every place in Australia has the two-dog rule. But we do."

"It isn't really fair," Ollie adds. "Families can have as many two-legs as they want."

Mick looks very sad.

"Don't worry, Mick," I say. "We'll find you a family. You'll see."

"Sure," Callie agrees. "There are plenty of families on Kangaroo Island with only one dog."

"Or with no dogs at all," Ollie adds.

What?

"That's just not right," I say. "Every family needs a dog."

"And every dog needs a family," Mick adds. He looks at me. "Do you think my mummy and sisters will find new families?"

"I bet they will," I say. Even though I don't really know.

"Then I'm going to find a new family, too," Mick tells Callie and Ollie. "Even if Sparky and I have to search the whole island!"

Gulp. This island seems pretty

big. We could be searching a long, long time.

Which means it could be a long, long time until I see Josh again.

I can't let that happen!

CHAPTER 4

"Look at all those birds!" I say a little while later.

Mick and I have wandered into a strange place. It's covered with blue-gray and white birds. They're everywhere.

Except in the sky. Which is weird. Where I come from, birds fly. But *these* birds walk.

I look over at Mick. He is watching a big bird walk beside a tiny bird.

That's funny. It looks like the big bird is wearing a coat. Sort of like the

coat Josh wears sometimes when he goes away with his friend Sophie.

I do not know why Josh likes wearing a coat. I do not know why birds would want to wear coats, either. I hate my coat. It makes my fur itch.

"Look at that baby penguin with his mum," Mick says quietly.

"A baby what?" I ask him.

"The little one is a baby penguin," Mick repeats. "And the big one must be his mother. They're a family. I can tell."

Hmmm . . .

"They're a family," I say slowly. "And you're looking for a family. So maybe . . ."

Mick gives me a funny look. "You

think I could be part of a penguin family?"

"Why not?" I answer. "I'm a dog, and Josh is a two-leg. We're not the same. But we're a family. Why can't dogs and birds be a family?"

Mick gets real quiet. Finally, he nods. "Sure," he says. "Why not?"

Mick runs over to the mother and baby penguin. He gives them a big, friendly grin. Then he asks, "Will you be my family?"

The mother and baby jump a little. They waddle away as fast as they can.

Mick stops smiling. "I don't think they want me," he says.

Poor Mick. I wish I could do something to make him happy.

I see a little white ball sitting in a hole. Nothing cheers up a dog like playing ball.

"Hey, Mick!" I cry out. "Do you want to play ball?"

Mick picks up his head. He doesn't look so sad now. "Sure!" he exclaims.

He runs over to where I am standing. He opens his mouth wide and gets ready to pick up the ball. And then . . .

Wiggle, waggle, wait a minute. What's happening? The ball is moving. *All by itself!*

"Crikey!" Mick cries out. "How'd you do that, Sparky?"

"Me?" I ask. "I didn't do anything."

"Then how . . . ," Mick begins. Suddenly, he stops talking and stares at the ball.

I'm staring, too. *Because now the ball is cracking open.*

Hey! There's something inside there.

Crack. Crack. Crack. There's a mouth. A little pointed mouth.

Crack. Crack. Crack. Now there's a face.

Crack. Crack. Crack.

Hey! It's a bird! A teeny, tiny penguin bird.

"Hello, little penguin," I bark to it. "That's a great trick. How did you get inside the ball?"

The penguin doesn't answer.

Haaa! Haaa!

But a bigger penguin sure does. She starts making *haaa*ing noises. Really, really *loud haaa*ing noises.

We don't need to speak penguin to know what she's saying.

"She wants us to get out of here," Mick says. He starts to run.

Haaa! Haaa!

That bird sure is loud. And her sharp mouth looks scary.

"Wait for me!" I call to Mick. "I'm coming with you!"

CHAPTER 5

Mick and I don't stop running until we reach a park with green grass and trees.

"I don't know why that big penguin didn't want us to play with the little penguin," I say.

"She probably thought we were going to hurt him," Mick says.

I shake my head. "We just wanted to play."

"She didn't know that," he says. "That baby penguin is lucky he has a mum to protect him. I wish . . ."

Mick is still talking, but I'm not listening. I can't listen to anything when my nose smells something yummy.

Sniffety, sniff, sniff.

Fish! I smell fish! It smells *yummy, yum, yum.* I just gotta have some.

My paws must smell it, too, because the next thing I know, they are running toward the smell.

Now I am standing by something very, very hot. And very, very smoky.

Mick runs up beside me.

"What kind of fish is that?" I wonder out loud.

"It's fish on the barbie," Mick replies.

"What's a barbie?" I ask him.

"You've never heard of a barbie?"

he asks. He sounds surprised. "It's a barbecue grill."

Barbecue! "Why didn't you say so?" I ask him. "I had barbecue meat in Texas. It was *yummy, yum, yum.*"

"I don't know where Texas is," Mick says. "But I bet they don't have anything as delicious as fish right off the barbie!"

I smile. "There's only one way to find out," I tell him.

I start to follow my nose. And Mick starts to follow me.

Sniffety, sniff, sniff. My nose leads me to a small group of two-legs.

I sure hope the two-legs here on Kangaroo Island are good sharers. That barbecue fish smells *yummy, yum, yum.*

I spot a little two-leg. She is sitting on the lap of a big two-leg.

Little two-legs are the best food sharers. They drop their food all the time! I sneak over and stand beside her.

Plop. Sure enough, a big piece of fish falls onto the ground. I scoop it up in my mouth!

Oh boy! This fish is delish!

I look up at the two-legs. They don't even notice me. They are too busy smiling. And laughing. They look really nice.

Hey . . .

"These two-legs could be your family, Mick!" I exclaim.

"Do you really think so?" Mick asks me.

"Sure," I say. "Two-legs make great families."

"I guess it's worth a try," Mick agrees.

I watch as my friend smiles up at the group of two-legs.

"G'day, mates!" Mick barks in his loudest voice. "Will you be my family?"

Mick leaps up to sit on the lap of
one of the big two-legs.

The big two-leg's eyes open wide.
His face turns bright red. He isn't
smiling anymore.

Uh-oh. That big two-leg does *not*
like having a dog on his lap!

The two-leg stands up.

Thump!

Mick falls off his lap. He tumbles to the ground!

"Crikey, mate!" Mick shouts at him. "That hurt!"

I don't get it. *Josh* always likes it when I jump onto his lap. He laughs and pets my head. But this two-leg is not laughing. He's not petting Mick on the head. Instead, he's waving his arms and shouting.

I do not have to speak two-leg to know what this one is saying. He doesn't want to be Mick's family.

"Let's go," I say to Mick.

The two-leg reaches toward the ground. Mick looks up at him.

Uh-oh. I think Mick is hoping the

angry two-leg will pick him up and take him home.

I don't think that will happen. Angry two-legs do not take dogs home. They take them to the *pound*.

"Come on, Mick," I bark. "That is not the right family for you."

"But . . . ," Mick starts.

"Trust me," I tell Mick. "Run! Now!"

I guess Mick trusts me. Because the next thing I know, Mick is running.

And so am I. My paws are moving. Fast. Faster. *Fastest.*

My paws have no idea where they are going. Neither do I. I just know we have to get out of here.

49

CHAPTER 6

Yikes.

I don't know where I am. All I know is it's dark in here. *Really* dark. *Scary* dark.

I can't see a thing!

Thumpety, thump, thump.

My heart is beating really, really hard. It must be scared of the dark, too. Which is weird, because my heart doesn't have eyes. It can't see even when it *isn't* dark.

I wonder if Mick has followed me into this dark, dark place.

I sure hope so. I don't want to be in here alone.

"Mick?" I call into the darkness.

"Sparky!" he shouts. "Am I glad to hear you."

"Not as glad as I am to hear *you*," I assure him.

I blink my eyes a few times. Now I can see—a little bit. And I don't see any two-legs at all. *Phew.*

But . . .

"Hey, that's weird," I say.

"What's weird?" Mick asks.

"Those rocks," I say. "They're hanging from the ceiling. That doesn't make any sense. Rocks are supposed to be on the ground."

"That *is* weird," Mick agrees. "I don't . . ."

Squeak. Squeak.

Mick stops talking.

"Did you hear that?" he asks me nervously.

Squeak. Squeak.

Gulp. There's someone in here with us. Someone who doesn't speak dog.

I wonder if that someone even *likes* dogs?

What if Mick and I are stuck in this dark place with a squeaky dog *hater*? This could be *baddy, bad, bad!*

Squeak. Squeak.

Mick turns around slowly. Then he smiles. "No worries, mate," he says. "It's just some birds hanging upside down from the ceiling."

Huh?

Birds don't hang upside down.

They don't squeak, either. Birds tweet.

I look up at the ceiling. *Hey!* Wait a minute.

"Those aren't birds," I tell Mick. "They're bats. I know. I met a bat once when I was in the Amazon Rain Forest."

"They look like birds," Mick says. "They have wings."

"Bats have wings, but they don't have feathers," I tell him. "They have fur. Just like dogs."

Hmmm. That gives me an idea.

"Maybe this is your new family," I say to Mick.

Mick shakes his head. "I don't know how to hang upside down."

"You could learn," I say. "Dogs are better than anyone when it comes to learning new tricks."

To prove it, I do *my* tricks: *Sit. Lie down. Roll over.*

"Did your Josh family teach you that?" Mick asks me.

"Yup!" I say.

"Do you teach Josh things?" Mick asks.

"Sure," I answer proudly. "I trained Josh to give me a treat every time I do a trick."

"Wow!" Mick says. "That's a good trick!"

"Maybe you can teach your new bat family to give you a treat whenever you hang upside down," I say.

"It's worth a try," Mick agrees. He looks up at the bats. "Will you be my family?" he asks them.

My heart is *thumpety, thump, thumping.* I hope the bats will be nice to Mick. I hope they won't yell or fly away.

The bats stay very still. They just keep hanging around, upside down.

"I bet they would like me better if I could hang upside down," Mick says.

"Give it a try," I tell him.

"Okay," Mick agrees. "First I have to get up on the ceiling."

Mick starts jumping as high as he can. But he does not reach the rocks.

"I'll never be able to do that," Mick says.

"Don't give up," I tell him. "You gotta—"

Just then, we hear a tiny bug buzzing in the air. Then a bat comes flying across the room.

Gulp. The bat swallows the bug.

"Crikey!" Mick exclaims. "What did that bat just do?"

"I think he ate the bug," I tell Mick.

"Bats eat bugs?" Mick asks me.

"I guess so," I say.

"Well, that's that," Mick says. "This is not the right family for me. Just imagine how many of those little bities I'd need to eat to fill my tummy!"

I think *bities* must mean *bugs*.

Mick is right. The bats aren't the right family for him. And this dark place with the hanging rocks isn't the right home for him, either. Because home is where you can *always* fill your tummy.

Grumble, rumble.

That's my tummy talking. And I know what it's saying, because I talk tummy.

"Come on, Mick," I say.

"Where are we going?" he asks me.

"I don't know," I admit. "But I sure hope wherever it is, there's food. Because I'm hungry!"

CHAPTER 7

"It's too bad my mummy isn't here," Mick says. "She always knows where to get food."

Poor Mick. He misses his old family so much.

I don't want him to be sad. I want to make him feel happy. But how? *Thinkety, think, think.*

I know! I will show him how to find food all by himself. Food always makes dogs happy!

"Do you want to learn how to find food?" I ask him.

"Yes!" Mick barks excitedly. "Can you show me?"

"Just follow your nose. Like I did when we found the fish on the barbie." I hold my head high in the air and *sniffety, sniff, sniff.* "Yum! Do you smell that?"

Mick holds his head high. He *sniffety, sniff, sniffs.* "I smell something sweet," he tells me.

"Yup!" I say. "Now all we have to do is walk toward the sweet smell. The stronger the smell, the closer we are to the food."

"Wow!" Mick says. "Did your Josh teach you that trick?"

I shake my head. "My nose

learned how to *sniffety, sniff, sniff* all on its own."

"Let me try!" Mick barks excitedly. He holds his head high and sniffs. "I think it's coming from over there."

That sweet stuff smells *yummy, yum, yum*. I gotta get some.

My paws start running. Fast. Faster. *Fastest!*

I am running so fast, my fur flies in my eyes. I can't see.

But my paws keep running. Fast. Faster . . . *CRASH!*

Uh-oh!

I feel something ooey and gooey flowing all over my paws.

Sniffety, sniff, sniff. That ooey-gooey stuff sure smells sweet.

I lick my paws. *Yummy, yum, yum!*

That ooey-gooey stuff is delicious. Some of my fur is stuck in it. But that's okay. A little fur in the food never hurt anybody.

"Mick!" I call to my friend. "I found the sweet stuff!"

Mick comes running over. He starts licking up the ooey-gooey sweet stuff that has dripped onto the ground.

"I'm happy to bog in!" he barks excitedly.

"To what?" I ask him.

"Bog in," he repeats. "You know. Eat it really fast!"

I didn't know. But now I do. And Mick is right. This is the kind of treat a dog can really bog into! *Yummy, yum . . .*

"You two are gonna get it!"

It's a dog's voice, and she doesn't sound happy.

"Wait until our two-leg finds out you knocked over his honey strainer," another dog says. "He's going to be mad."

I turn around. There are two huge border collies standing behind us.

"Our two-leg doesn't like anyone touching his honey strainer," the first collie says.

"I think you better go home," the second collie says.

Mick's tail droops. His ears fall. "I *want* to go home. But I can't," he says.

The border collies both give him a funny look.

"Mick is trying to find a new home and a new family," I explain. I walk over and sniff their butts to say hello. "By the way, my name is Sparky."

"I'm Matilda," the first collie says. "And this is my sister Phoebe."

Phoebe sniffs Mick's butt to say hello. "Why can't you get home, Mick?" she asks.

"The giant puddle is too big for me to swim across," Mick explains.

Phoebe and Matilda both give him another funny look. I don't think they have any idea what he's talking about.

"How about you, Sparky?" Phoebe asks. "Are you looking for a family, too?"

"I have a home and a family," I say. "But I sure would like more of this ooey-gooey sweet stuff . . ."

"That could take a while," Matilda says. "You have to wait for the bees to make more honey."

I have no idea what they're talking about.

"I have to wait for the *what* to make more *what*?" I ask.

"The bees," Matilda repeats. "They live over there, in the hives. It's their job to turn nectar from flowers into sweet, sticky honey."

I turn around and look for a bee house. But all I see is a bunch of big yellow blobs.

"This stuff is delicious," Mick says as he licks some honey off his paw. "I would eat it for brekkie, lunch, and supper if I could."

"Maybe you can," I tell Mick. "If the bees were your family, they could feed you honey all day long."

"I reckon you're right, Sparky!" Mick says excitedly.

"I reckon Sparky's *wrong*," Matilda warns Mick. "You can't be part of a bee family."

"Why can't he?" I ask her.

"Well, for one thing, Mick's too big to fit inside the hive," Phoebe says. "And for another . . ."

Mick and I don't hear the rest of what Phoebe says. We're already standing next to the bee house. Mick is looking for a family. I'm just looking for more of that ooey-gooey sweet honey stuff.

As soon as we get close to the

yellow bee house, Mick puts on his friendliest doggie smile.

"Will you be my family?" he asks the bees.

At least that's what I *think* he is asking. It's hard to hear over the weird *buzz, buzz, buzzing* noise coming from the bee house.

BUZZZZZZZZ!

Suddenly, the noise gets really loud. And then . . .

OUCH! Something stings me. Right on the ear!

"Owie!" Mick yelps.

I guess something has stung him, too!

"I told you the bees weren't a family you would want to be a part of," Matilda barks.

"Bees are mean," Phoebe adds. "Especially when they're mad."

BUZZZZ!

OUCH! The bees are definitely mad now. One just stung me on my *bee*-hind.

I'm not waiting around for any more ooey-gooey sweet stuff. It's not worth it.

"Come on, Mick," I bark over all the buzzing. "It's time to *bee*-t it!"

CHAPTER 8

"It's weird the way someone so mean can make something so sweet," I say to Mick a few minutes later.

We are far, far away from the bees. But I still have a little bit of ooey-gooey honey stuck to my paws. I lick it off. There's dirt and fur mixed in. But it's still yummy!

"My leg hurts where a bee stung me," Mick says. "I wish my mummy were here. She would lick it and make it all better."

"A mummy can do that?" I ask him.

"Sure," Mick tells me. "A mummy can do anything. If you're cold, she can cuddle with you until you're warm. And if you're tired, she can lie down and let you rest right on top of her."

"Like a dog bed?" I ask him.

"Better," Mick tells me. "Much better."

Wow. That mummy thing sounds *wiggle, waggle, wonderful*!

"You can't rest on top of a mummy bee," Mick says. "She might sting."

Thump. Thump. Thump. Thump.

Something is thumping on the ground behind us. I turn around.

What is that?

It could be a two-leg.

Or maybe a four-leg.

I'm not sure.

It's standing on just two paws. Like a two-leg does.

But it has a long tail. And fur. Like a four-leg does.

"What is that?" I ask Mick.

"A kangaroo," Mick tells me.

Well, that makes sense. After all, this place is called Kangaroo Island.

"Is a kangaroo a two-leg or a . . ." I stop in the middle of my sentence.

Wiggle, waggle, what just happened?

"Did you see that?" I ask Mick.

"What?" Mick asks.

"The big kangaroo has a little one attached to it," I say. "See? He's sticking his head out of her belly."

Mick laughs. "That's a joey," he tells me.

"How do you know his name?" I ask.

Mick laughs again. "His name's not Joey. He *is* a joey: a baby kangaroo. The big kangaroo must be his mummy. She's carrying him in her pouch."

"In her *what*?" I ask.

"That pocket on her belly," Mick explains. "Where he stays warm and safe. She feeds him in there, too."

Hmmm . . .

Mick is a really small puppy.

No bigger than the kangaroo in that pouch.

"That's it!" I shout.

"What's it?" Mick asks me.

"You can join a kangaroo family," I tell him. "You can ride around in a pouch and be all warm and safe."

Mick looks over at a group of kangaroos that has gathered near us.

"I *am* tired," he says finally. "It would feel nice to be carried for a while."

"There are lots of little kangaroos in pouches," I tell him. "You would have plenty of puppies to play with."

"Joeys," Mick corrects me.

"Whatever you call them," I say, "you would be able to play together."

"That's true," Mick agrees.

I watch as Mick slowly pads over to a big kangaroo.

"Will you be my family?" he asks her.

The kangaroo looks down at him. But she doesn't answer. I guess that's because kangaroos don't speak dog.

Mick looks over at me sadly. But I can't let him give up.

"Get into her pouch," I call to him. "It's all warm and safe in there, remember?"

Mick jumps up high. He tries to dive into the kangaroo's pouch.

Plop.

He misses and falls to the ground.

The kangaroo looks surprised. She hops backward and bangs into another kangaroo. He was sleeping

82

on the ground. But he's awake now.

Boing! The used-to-be-sleeping kangaroo jumps up, surprised.

Then he turns around and spots another kangaroo staring at him. He bashes him with his tail.

The kangaroo doesn't like that. *Pow!* He punches back with his paw.

Suddenly, there's a whole lot of jumping, punching, kicking, and tail-bashing going on.

"Mick!" I shout. "Get out of there! You're gonna get stomped on!"

Punch!

Mick slips right between the two fighting kangaroos.

Kick!

He leaps out of the way of a kangaroo paw.

Bash!

He darts out of the path of a swinging kangaroo tail.

"This is NOT the family for me!" Mick says, and he runs over to me.

"Definitely not," I agree. "They fight too much."

Mick looks over at the joeys inside their mothers' pouches. His tail sinks. His ears flatten.

"I didn't find a family here," he whimpers. "I haven't found one anywhere. I wonder if I ever will."

Mick is so sad. But I don't know what to say. I'm wondering the same thing.

"Maybe I should try to get back on the metal machine that floats in the giant puddle," Mick says. "If I'm lucky, it will take me back to where I came from."

"Why would you want to go there?" I ask him. "Your mummy and sisters aren't at the bridge anymore."

"There are lots of dogs back where I came from," Mick answers. "And they don't have any rules about how many dogs can live in one family."

"But the dogcatcher could still be looking for you," I remind him.

Mick doesn't answer. He's already run off toward the big puddle.

I have to stop him! I can't let Mick go back to his old home. Not when there's a dogcatcher on the loose!

CHAPTER 9

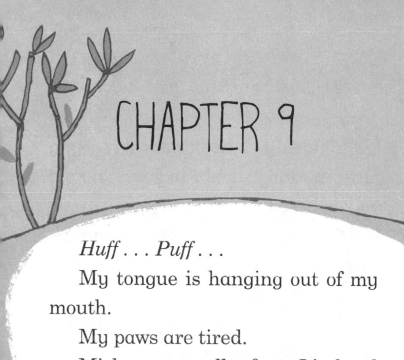

Huff . . . Puff . . .

My tongue is hanging out of my mouth.

My paws are tired.

Mick runs really fast. It's hard to keep up with him. But I have to stop him from getting on that metal machine.

Except . . .

There's no metal machine here. There's nothing but water. Lots and lots of water.

"Hey. Where did you two come from?"

Suddenly, I hear another dog. I turn around quickly to see a big old mixed-breed.

"I've never seen you two ankle-biters on Kangaroo Island before," the dog tells me.

"I don't bite," I tell him. "Biting is bad. Unless you're biting into a hunk of meat, of course."

"He just means we're puppies," Mick explains. "Ankle-biter is another word for a little two-leg. Or in our case, puppy four-legs."

"You'd better get back to your families," the old mixed-breed says.

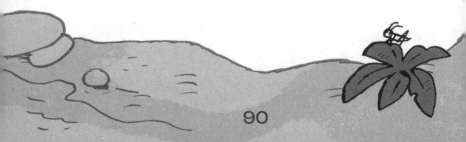

Mick lies down on the ground. He buries his head in his paws.

"What's with him?" the old mixed-breed asks me.

"He doesn't actually *have* a family anymore," I tell him. "We've been trying to find him a new one all day."

"I'm a pup all alone in the world," Mick groans.

"Pup . . . ," the old mixed-breed repeats slowly. "That gives me an idea. I might know a great family for you. One with lots of pups."

"But there can only be two pups in a family on Kangaroo Island," I say.

"Two *dog* pups," the old mixed-breed says. "But I didn't say these pups were dogs, did I?"

94

CHAPTER 10

"What are those things?" I ask the old mixed-breed a few minutes later. We are standing in front of a large group of really big . . . I don't know what.

They have fur like dogs. But they have whiskers like cats.

They have things that look like paws, only they are huge and flat.

Some of these creatures are playing in the sand. Others are playing in the giant water bowl.

"They're sea lions," the old mixed-breed tells us.

"The little ones look like they're having fun," I point out to Mick.

"Sea-lion pups love to play—in and out of the water," the old mixed-breed says.

Bark! Bark!

The sea lions are barking! I don't know what they're saying, but they are definitely barking.

Two of the sea-lion pups are sitting on a rock, eating a fish. Just watching them makes me hungry.

Mick must be hungry, too, because he runs right over to the two pups and sniffs at the fish.

The sea-lion pups jump back, surprised. And then . . . they move over so Mick can take a bite!

I guess sea lions are good sharers.

Mick eats really fast. So do the sea lions. In a flash, the fish is all gone.

The sea-lion pups waddle toward the water.

Bark! Bark!

The sea lions are barking again. I do not understand what they are saying.

But Mick seems to understand. Because he walks over to the edge of the water. And then . . .

Mick starts swimming! Just like the sea-lion pups!

Uh-oh! Suddenly, one of the sea-lion pups disappears. I can't see him anywhere.

"Where did that pup go?" I ask the

old mixed-breed. "Is he buried under the water?"

"Just watch," he says calmly.

So I watch. A minute later, the pup's head pops up. He's holding a fish in his mouth!

The two sea-lion pups and Mick start swimming toward us. When they get back on land, they all start

eating the fish.

"The sea-lion pup was just getting food," the old mixed-breed explains. "There are a lot of fish in the water."

That means Mick will have a lot to eat—if the sea lions let him join their family.

Waddle, waddle, waddle. A huge

sea lion waddles over to where Mick and the sea-lion pups are eating.

"Who's that?" I ask the old mixed-breed.

"That's their mother," he tells me.

The mother sea lion looks at Mick.

Mick looks back at the mother sea lion.

Gulp.

I hope the mother sea lion isn't angry that Mick is there. Because the sea-lion mother is huge. If she wanted to, she could crush Mick!

I'm really scared.

But Mick isn't. He moves in close and rubs against her.

The mother sea lion looks down and nuzzles Mick's fur. That seems kind of like what Josh does to me

when I crawl up on his lap.

Suddenly, I hear a funny noise. It sounds a little like barking and a little like laughing. It's coming from the two sea-lion pups. They are climbing on top of their mother.

They look like puppies playing.

The next thing I know, Mick is scrambling up onto the mother sea lion's back.

Bark! Bark!

The sea-lion pups bark happily as they slide down from their mother and land on the ground.

"Whee!" Mick shouts as he slides with them. "This is fun!"

The sea-lion pups waddle back to the water. Mick runs beside them.

Whoosh. The sea-lion pups dive underwater.

Whoosh. Mick dives underwater.

One sea-lion pup pops up. He has a fish in his mouth.

The other sea-lion pup pops up. He has a fish in *his* mouth.

Then Mick . . .

Wiggle, waggle, uh-oh.

Mick *isn't* popping up. I don't see him anywhere.

My heart starts *thumpety, thump,*

thumping. Where is he?

Bark! Bark!

The sea-lion pups start barking really loud.

The mother sea lion waddles toward the water.

She starts swimming fast. Faster. *Fastest.*

Then she dives under the water. And a minute later . . .

There's Mick! And he's got a fish in his mouth!

I watch as the sea-lion mother helps push Mick out of the water and onto the sand.

My tail starts wagging. It's very happy. My tail knows that Mick has found his family.

The best part is Mick didn't even have to ask to be part of the sea-lion family. *He just fit right in.*

Seeing Mick with his family makes me miss *my* family. It's time for me to go home.

"I have to leave, Mick!" I shout.

"Hooroo, Sparky!" Mick shouts to me. "And thanks."

Hooroo is another one of Mick's funny words. But this time I think I know what it means.

Good-bye.

"Hooroo, mate!" I shout back to Mick. "Have fun with your family!"

CHAPTER 11

Diggety, dig, dig. I am digging a big hole near the tree where I buried my bone. Dirt is flying everywhere.

Snort!

The fluffy koala still doesn't like having me near his tree.

Diggety, dig, dig—

There it is! My magic bone. Right where I left it.

SNORT!

Now the koala is getting really mad. He shakes the tree branches. Pink flowers fall from the tree.

"Okay!" I shout up to him. "I'm leaving."

I open my mouth and . . . *CHOMP!*

Wiggle, waggle, whew. I feel dizzy—like my insides are spinning all around—but my outsides are standing still. Stars are twinkling in front of my eyes—even though it's daytime! All around me I smell food—fried chicken, salmon, roast beef. But there isn't any food in sight.

Kaboom! Kaboom! Kaboom!

I'm still standing under a tree.

I look up. There's still something furry up in the branches.

Uh-oh. What if my bone didn't take me home this time? What if I'm stuck in . . .

Meow!

Hey! Wait a minute. That's not an angry koala.

That's an angry *cat!*

It's Queenie the meanie, our neighborhood cat.

My bone brought me home, just like I wanted it to!

"Go away, Queenie the meanie!" I bark.

Hiss!

Queenie bares her claws at me. She leaps from the tree branch and lands on top of my fence. Then she disappears on the other side.

I like when Queenie disappears.

Now I'm all alone in my yard. But not for long. Josh will be home soon. And I will be here waiting for him.

I run to the back of the yard, where the flowers are. I drop my bone in the hole I left there. Then I push the dirt back over the bone. It is buried. No one will know it is there—except me, of course.

Vroom. Vroom.

That's the sound of Josh's metal machine with four round paws.

Suddenly, the gate opens.

My Josh is home!

"Hi, Josh! Hi, Josh!" I bark. "Do you wanna play? Do you? Do you?"

Josh bends down and pets my head. He picks something off my fur. Then he gives me a funny look.

Josh is holding a pink flower. It must have landed on my fur when the koala shook those tree branches.

I wish I could tell Josh about Kangaroo Island, where I got that flower.

I wish I could explain how my new friend Mick found himself a family.

But I can't.

Josh bends down and picks up a ball that is sitting in the grass. He starts to throw it.

Uh-oh!

"No, Josh!" I bark. "Not the ball!"

I run over to the tree and pick up a big stick. I run back and drop the stick at Josh's feet.

"Throw the stick!" I bark. "It's safer. Baby penguins do not hide inside sticks."

So Josh throws the stick. And I run after it. My tail wags. Playing with Josh always makes me happy.

Josh may not speak dog, but he understands a lot about me. And I understand a lot about him.

I guess that's what happens when you're part of a family.

Fun Facts about Sparky's Adventures in Australia

Kangaroo Island

This is Australia's third-largest island. Almost one-third of the island is used for wildlife sanctuaries—places where birds and animals are kept safe from hunters.

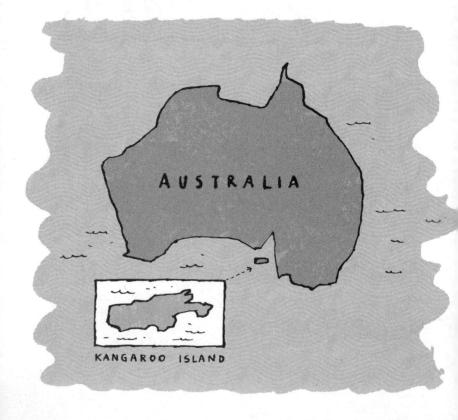

KANGAROO ISLAND

Koalas

These furry creatures may look like bears, but they are actually in the same family as kangaroos. Koalas have sharp claws that help them climb trees. They only eat one food: the leaves of the eucalyptus tree.

Little Blue Penguins

Australia's little blue penguins are the smallest of all the penguin species. They cannot fly, but they are great swimmers. That's lucky, because penguins eat fish that they catch in the ocean, and they drink salty seawater, too!

Kelly Hill Caves

These underground caves are famous for the rock formations that hang from the ceilings. The Kelly Hill Caves are home to many animals, including bats, frogs, and owls.

Ligurian Bees

Kangaroo Island was named a bee sanctuary more than 130 years ago. That keeps the bees on the island safe from the pesticides that kill off other types of bees. Each year tourists make special trips to visit the honey farms of Kangaroo Island, just to taste the sweet treat created by Ligurian bees.

Kangaroos

Kangaroos travel in groups called mobs. When kangaroo babies are born, they are tiny and cannot walk or eat on their own. So they stay in their mothers' pouches where they are carried and fed. When the joeys are about four months old, they start to take short walks on their own.

If adult kangaroos are threatened, they can use their feet to kick and their upper paws to swipe and punch. This makes it look like they are boxing.

Australian Sea Lions

This rare type of sea lion can be found living in big groups at Kangaroo Island's Seal Bay Conservation Park. They find fish to eat in the shallow water near the shore. Mother sea lions not only raise their own young, but they have also been known to take care of other pups that may have been abandoned.

About the Author

Nancy Krulik is the author of more than 200 books for children and young adults, including three *New York Times* Best Sellers. She is best known for being the author and creator of several successful book series for children, including Katie Kazoo, Switcheroo; How I Survived Middle School; and George Brown, Class Clown. Nancy lives in Manhattan with her husband, composer Daniel Burwasser, and her crazy beagle mix, Josie, who manages to drag her along on many exciting adventures without ever leaving Central Park.

About the Illustrator

You could fill a whole attic with Seb's drawings! His collection includes some very early pieces made when he was four—there is even a series of drawings he did at the movies in the dark! When he isn't doodling, he likes to make toys and sculptures, as well as bows and arrows for his two boys, Oscar and Leo, and their numerous friends. Seb is French and lives in England. His website is www.sebastienbraun.com.

31901059424376